W9-AHT-586

AR:3.4/05
3-07   X
NEB

20.8.96

My Mom Loves Me More Than Sushi

by Filomena Gomes

illustrated by Ashley Spires

Second
Story
Press

My mom loves me more than **sushi**.

While the rolls squirt and squish out of my chopsticks, she easily brings the fish and sticky rice to her lips and smiles with her eyes closed.

M
0729 03/07/07 NEB
s, Filomena, 1965-

om loves me more than
hi

LEROY COLLINS LEON COUNTY
PUBLIC LIBRARY SYSTEM
200 West Park Avenue
Tallahassee, Florida 32301-7720

My mom loves me more than biscotti.

I dunk my cookie in milk and she dunks hers in coffee, and then we let the moon tips melt in our mouths.

My mom loves me more than **houska bread.**

We mash and braid the yellow dough with our bare hands, layer the braids to make a sculpture, and then wait forever for it to bake. Then we tear it apart and nibble it like mice.

My mom loves me more than canja. When it's cold out she makes soup from chicken, throws in rice, and I get to add lemon juice and mint leaves. As I slurp, it warms me right up to my earlobes.

Portugal

My mom loves me more than **couscous**.

Saying "Mmmmmm," she pours rosewater over a bowl of steaming wheat. The tiny grains tickle my throat.

My mom loves me more than **megadarra**.

The house smells like spices and onions when she makes big giant piles of lentils and rice. I always scoop yogurt and peppermint on top.

Egypt

My mom loves me more than **smorgastarta**.

Just like a house, we build a huge sandwich cake out of bread and mayonnaise. Then we decorate the top and sides with cucumber, lettuce, tomatoes and smoked salmon.

Sweden

My mom loves me more than **crepes**.

In the morning the buttery smell calls me from my warm and comfy bed, and we roll very thin pancakes full of yummy treats like fruit and cream.

My mom loves me more than jambalaya.

While we dance to crazy music, she mixes tomatoes, peppers, rice and shrimp and a LOT of garlic. The final touch is spicy sausage, which makes my eyes water every time.

My mom loves me more than **samosas.**

She folds and stuffs fat triangles with vegetables or meat. It is my job to arrange the colored sauces called chutney. I like to set them up like a traffic light: green, yellow and red.

India and Pakistan

My mom loves me more than
sushi
biscotti
houska
canja
couscous
megadarra
smorgastarta
crepes
jambalaya and
samosas.

And I love my mom more than anything, too, because we learn about these fabulous foods from around the world — together!

à Madeleine, Zachary et Éva Simone
je vous aime plus que le sushi
— F.G.

To Megs and Ethan and their love of new food
— A.S.

LIBRARY AND ARCHIVES CANADA CATALOGUING IN PUBLICATION

Gomes, Filomena, 1965-
My mom loves me more than sushi / by Filomena Gomes ; illustrated by Ashley Spires.

ISBN 1-897187-09-2 (bound)
ISBN 1-897187-13-0 (pbk.)

I. Spires, Ashley, 1978- II. Title.

PS8613.O44M9 2006   jC813'.6   C2006-901231-8

Text copyright © 2006 by Filomena Gomes
Illustrations copyright © 2006 by Ashley Spires
First published in the USA in 2007
Designed by Melissa Kaita
Printed in China by Everbest Company Ltd.

Second Story Press gratefully acknowledges the support of the Ontario Arts Council and the Canada Council for the Arts for our publishing program. We acknowledge the financial support of the Government of Canada through the Book Publishing Industry Development Program.

Published by
SECOND STORY PRESS
20 Maud Street, Suite 401
Toronto, Ontario, Canada
M5V 2M5

www.secondstorypress.ca